Enid Blyton ™

The Talking

Illustrated by Pam Storey

Once there was a little girl called Jennifer. She walked a mile to school each day and back, and that was quite a long way. Sometimes it rained and then she took her mac. Sometimes it was cold and she took her coat and sometimes it was very hot and she wore no coat at all, but a shady hat in case she got sunstroke.

One day she set out in the sunshine. It was a nice, sunny, autumn day. Jennifer had a short coat on and her lace-up shoes and her school hat. She ran along, singing a song she was learning at school.

Half-way to school a great black cloud came up and it began to pour with rain. How it poured! You should have seen it. The rain came down like slanting lines of silver and big puddles came all along the road.

Jennifer stood under a tree to shelter herself. When the rain stopped she ran out into the road again – and stepped right into a most enormous puddle! It was deeper than her ankles – so she wet her shoes and socks dreadfully.

"Good gracious!" said Jennifer, in dismay. "Now look what I've done! I shall have to sit in school with wet shoes and socks all morning, and I shall get an awful cold."

She walked along very sadly, thinking of how she would sneeze and cough the next day and then she passed by a little yellow cottage where a dear old lady lived all alone. The old lady was shaking the crumbs off her tablecloth for the birds in the garden and she called to Jennifer, who knew her well.

"Did you get caught in that rainstorm, my dear?"

"Yes, I did," said Jennifer sadly. "And just look at my shoes and socks! I stepped into a puddle, and now they are wet through!"

"Dear me, that's very dangerous," said the old woman at once. "Come along in and I'll see if I can lend you a pair of my stockings and a dry pair of shoes. I have a very small foot, so maybe I can manage something for you."

So Jennifer went into the tidy little cottage and the old lady found a pair of lace-up shoes for Jennifer and a pair of stockings.

"There!" she said. "These will do nicely. I can lend you a pair of

5

garters, too, to keep up the stockings. Put them on, my dear, and I will dry your wet things and have them ready for you by the time you pass by at dinner-time."

Jennifer put on the stockings. Then she put on the shoes. They had big tongues to them and long laces, but they were most comfortable. They felt nice and dry too.

"Thank you," said Jennifer gratefully. "I'll try not to tread in any more puddles with these on."

She skipped off to school. The old lady stood at the gate and called after her. "Oh, Jennifer! Just a minute. Don't be naughty at school today, will you? You may be sorry if you are!"

"How funny!" thought Jennifer. "Why should I have to be specially good today? I don't know."

Jennifer was not very good at school. She whispered and talked when she shouldn't. She made a mess in her writing book instead of keeping it nice and tidy. She pulled the plaits of the little girl in front and she pinched the boy next to her because she didn't like him. So you see, she really wasn't a very good child at school.

She didn't see any real reason why she should be good that day. So she didn't try. She picked up her number book so roughly that a page tore in half.

Then a funny thing happened. A voice spoke in the silence of the classroom – a rather deepdown, husky voice that no one had ever heard before.

"Careless girl, isn't she?" said the voice. "Did you see how she tore her number book?"

"Yes, I did," said another voice, just as deepdown and husky. "She ought to lose a mark for that."

"Who is talking?" asked Miss Brown in astonishment. Jennifer went red. How dare somebody talk about her like that?

She wondered if it was the little boy next to her. She pinched him slyly. A voice spoke loudly again.

"Did you see Jennifer pinch the boy next to her? Isn't she cruel?"

"A most un-kind child," said the second voice. "I don't think I like her."

"Oh! Who's talking like that about me!" cried Jennifer in a rage.

"It sounds like some body on the ground," said Miss Brown, puzzled and alarmed. Everyone looked on the floor. Nobody was hiding beneath the tables or desks.

Have you guessed what it was that was talking? Perhaps you have! It was the tongues in the two borrowed shoes! They chattered away to one another, and were most surprising to hear.

"I think she has a very cross face, don't you?" said one tongue. "It's a pity she doesn't look in the mirror. Then she would see how horrid she looks when she keeps frowning."

"Will you stop talking, whoever it is?" cried Miss Brown, and she rapped on her desk.

The shoes held their tongues and stopped talking for a while. They were frightened of Miss Brown. The class settled down to write. They were

copying from the blackboard. Jennifer did not try very hard. When she opened her desk to get out her pen her book slid to the floor.

"Good gracious!" said one tongue to the other. "Just look at Jennifer's dreadful writing! Did you ever see anything so awful for a child of ten? Really, she ought to be ashamed of herself."

"Perhaps she can't write any better," said the other, flapping a little.

"Look at that mistake! If I were the teacher, I'd put her into the corner."

"Oh! Oh!" cried Jennifer, stamping her foot and bursting into tears. "I won't stand it! Who is saying these horrid things about me?"

"I can't imagine, Jenny," said Miss Brown. "All I can say is that the things are perfectly true! It is a shocking thing that a girl of ten should write so badly and be so untidy."

Jennifer picked up her book sulkily and put it on her desk. The shoes chatted together again.

"She's got her horrid, sulky face on now. Isn't she a most unpleasant child? I wonder how many mistakes she will make on her next page!"

Jennifer set her teeth and made up her mind to make no mistakes at all. She wrote a really beautiful page and showed it to Miss Brown.

"Good gracious, Jennifer! I've never seen such nice writing from you before!" cried Miss Brown.

"You see, she can do it if she tries," said one shoe. "She's just too lazy to do it always."

"I'm not lazy, I'm not lazy!" cried Jennifer and she stamped her foot. That gave the shoes such a shock that they said nothing at all for a whole hour. Then it was

geography, a lesson that Jennifer didn't like. She leaned over and pulled the hair of the little girl in front of her. The little girl squealed.

"Somebody pulled my hair!" she cried.

Miss Brown looked up crossly.

"Was it you, Jenny?" she asked.

"No, Miss Brown," said Jennifer untruthfully.

"OooooooooOOOOOH!" said one shoe to the other. "Isn't she untruthful? Really! Ooooooooh!"

"Untruthful, cowardly and unkind," said the other shoe. "Why doesn't somebody send her to bed?"

Jennifer glared round at everyone, thinking somebody must be playing a trick on her, talking like this. But everyone was as astonished as she was.

"Who is talking?" cried Miss Brown, quite alarmed again. "I don't like this. I shall put the talkers into the corner if I hear any more."

"Fancy! She'd put us in the corner!" giggled a shoe. "Well, she'd have to put Jenny there, too, if she puts us."

"Perhaps we'd better not talk," said the other shoe. "I believe we are disturbing the class a little. Shhh!"

So they said no more until it was time to go home. Then Jennifer went sulkily to the cloakroom and took down her hat and coat. Another child got in her way and she gave him a push that knocked him right over.

"Isn't she rough?" said the shoe, shocked. "Did you see her push that nice little boy right over? If she did that to me, I'd kick her!"

"And I'd trip her up!" said the other shoe fiercely. "What a horrid girl!

Do you suppose anyone in the world likes her at all?"

"I expect her mother does," said the first shoe. "Mothers are funny – they always love their children even when the children are horrid and rude to them. I should think Jennifer is rude to her mother, wouldn't you?"

Jenny sat down on a bench and began to cry. "I'm not rude to my mother, I'm not, I'm not!" she wept. "I love her. I'm kind to her. Oh, who is it saying these unkind things about me? I may behave horribly sometimes, but I can be good when I try!"

"I don't believe that, do you?" said one shoe.

"No," said the other. "She couldn't be good! She's one of these spoilt children we've heard about."

The other children laughed. They were very sorry for Jennifer, but they couldn't help thinking that it would do her good to hear these things. She went off, crying bitterly, puzzled and unhappy.

The shoes talked on and on. They chatted about Jenny's bad writing and her wrong sums and her pinching and pushing. Jenny sobbed and cried all the way to the little yellow cottage. The old lady was waiting for her at the gate.

"Dear, dear!" she said, when she saw Jennifer coming along with red eyes and tear-stained cheeks. "What's the matter? Have those shoes been wagging their tongues too much?"

"Shoes? Wagging their tongues?" said Jenny in amazement. "Whatever do you mean?"

"Well, those shoes I lent you this morning can be most tiresome," said the old lady. "They belonged to my great-grandmother, you know, and were made by a brownie, so it is said. They have tongues, of course, just as your own lace-up shoes have – but these shoe tongues can talk – and talk they do! They are real chatterboxes. I hope they didn't say anything unkind!"

"Oh, no, we only spoke the truth!" cried the two shoe tongues together and they flapped themselves about in the shoes. Jennifer looked down in amazement. She took off the shoes very quickly indeed.

"So they were the talkers!" she said. "The tongues of my shoes! Well
– I never knew shoe tongues could talk!"

"Oh, my dear, they all could at one time," said the old lady. "That is
why they were called tongues, you know, because they spoke. But they did
say the silliest, most tiresome things, so now very few of them are allowed
to talk. I can't stop the tongues in this pair of shoes, though. That's why
I called to you to be good this morning – because I knew the shoe tongues
would talk about it if you were naughty."

"I shan't be quite so naughty in future," said Jenny, beginning to smile.

"I don't like to be thought lazy and stupid and horrid. Lend me your shoes in a month's time and see if they can say heaps of nice things about me for a change, will you?"

"Certainly," said the old lady, slipping Jenny's own shoes back on the girl's feet. "How cross they will be if there is nothing naughty they can chat about!"

I'd like to hear what they say in a month's time, wouldn't you? What would your shoe tongues say if they could speak, I wonder? Do tell me!